Cock-a-doodle-doo! Farmyard Hullabaloo

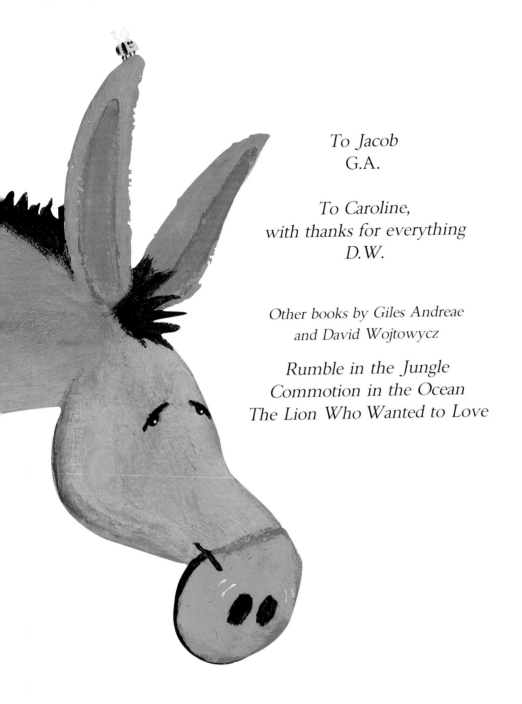

To Jacob
G.A.

To Caroline,
with thanks for everything
D.W.

*Other books by Giles Andreae
and David Wojtowycz*

*Rumble in the Jungle
Commotion in the Ocean
The Lion Who Wanted to Love*

ORCHARD BOOKS
96 Leonard Street, London EC2A 4XD
Orchard Books Australia
Unit 31/56 O'Riordan Street, Alexandria, NSW 2015
1 84362 068 5
First published in Great Britain in 1999
First paperback edition published in 2000
This edition published in 2002
Text © Purple Enterprises Ltd 1999
Illustrations © David Wojtowycz 1999
The right of Giles Andreae to be identified as the author and
David Wojtowycz as the illustrator of this work has been asserted by them
in accordance with the Copyright, Designs and Patents Act, 1988.
A CIP catalogue for this book is available from the British Library
4 6 8 10 9 7 5 3
Printed in Dubai

Cock-a-doodle-doo!
Farmyard Hullabaloo

Giles Andreae

Illustrated by
David Wojtowycz

ORCHARD BOOKS

Early in the morning
As the sun begins to rise,
The pigs are feeling hungry
And they're snorting in their sties.

The rooster wakes the farm up
With a cock-a-doodle-doo!
The sheepdog won't stop barking,
And the cows begin to moo.

There's a stomping in the stables
And there's bleating in the barn,
So let's climb aboard the tractor
And explore this noisy farm.

Rooster

Cock-a-doodle-doo!
Cock-a-doodle-doo!
I'm the rockin' rooster, baby,
Tell me, who are you?

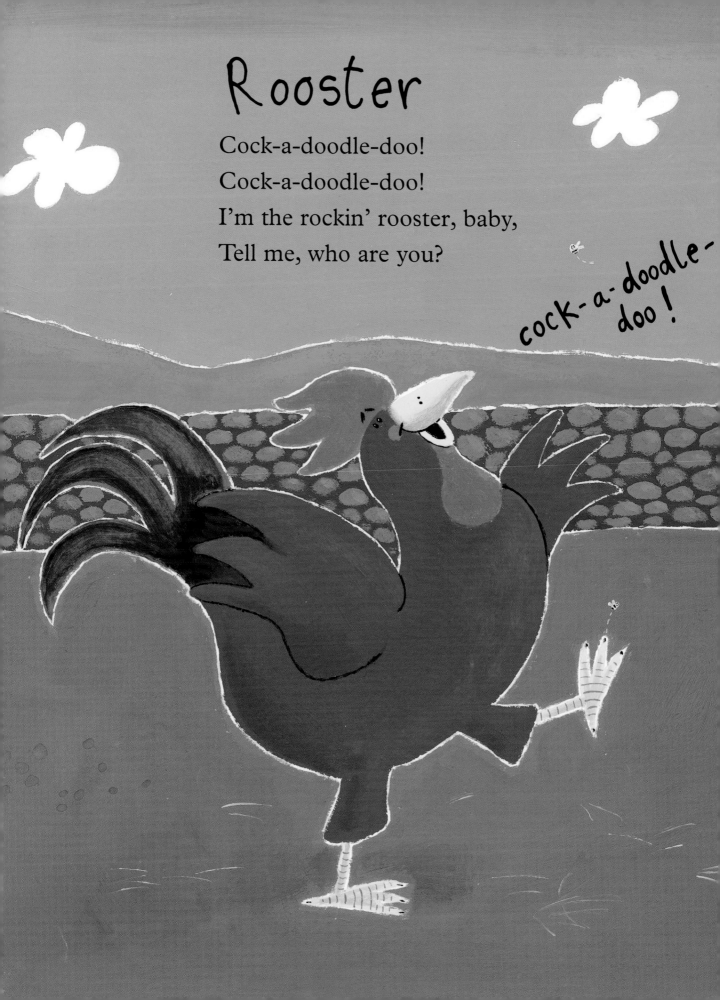

Chickens

We chickens are covered with feathers
All over our wings and our legs,
So of course we could fly
If we wanted to try
But we're too busy laying these eggs.

Cow

Sometimes I moo while I'm chewing
I hope you don't think that it's rude,
But mooing and chewing
Are what I like doing.
Do you moo when you chew your food?

moooooo!

Sheepdog

I am the farmer's old sheepdog,
His faithful and loyal best friend.
I've been by his side from the day I was born
And I'll stay with him right to the end.

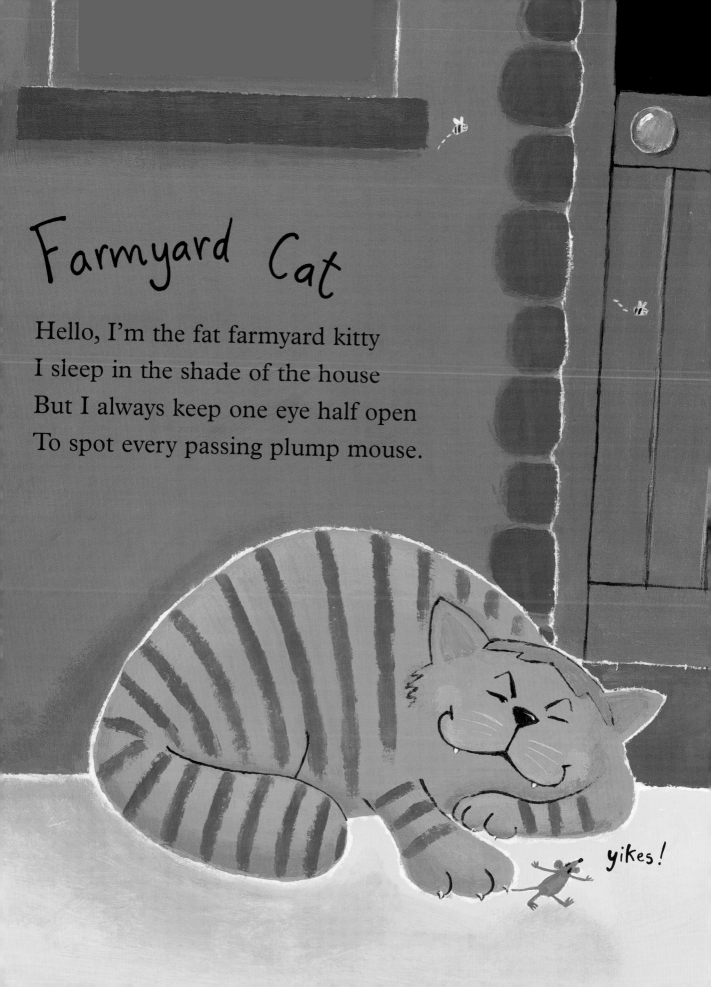

Farmyard Cat

Hello, I'm the fat farmyard kitty
I sleep in the shade of the house
But I always keep one eye half open
To spot every passing plump mouse.

yikes!

Pigs

I love looking after my piglets
And watching them wriggle and squeal.
They clamber all over each other all day
To snuffle around for a meal.

wriggle
wriggle

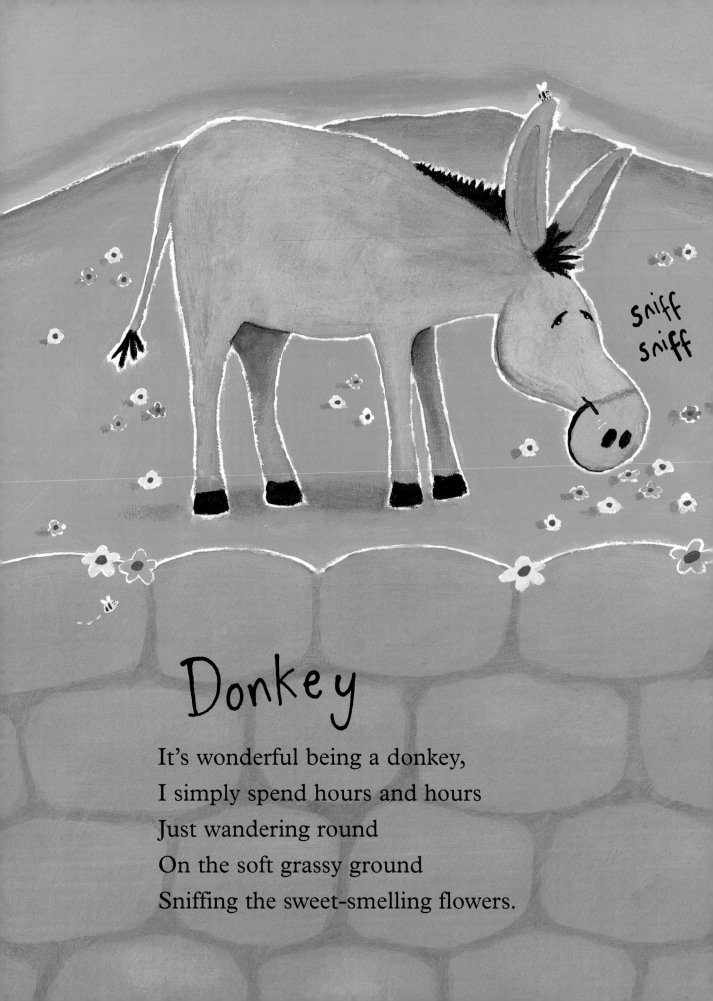

Donkey

It's wonderful being a donkey,
I simply spend hours and hours
Just wandering round
On the soft grassy ground
Sniffing the sweet-smelling flowers.

Turkey

I've got these funny, floppy things
That hang down from my neck,
They dangle when I gobble
And they wobble when I peck.

gobble

gobble

Geese

We waddle about in the paddock
And make such a din when we talk
That we sound like a bunch of old ladies
Who gossip and cackle and squawk.

cackle!

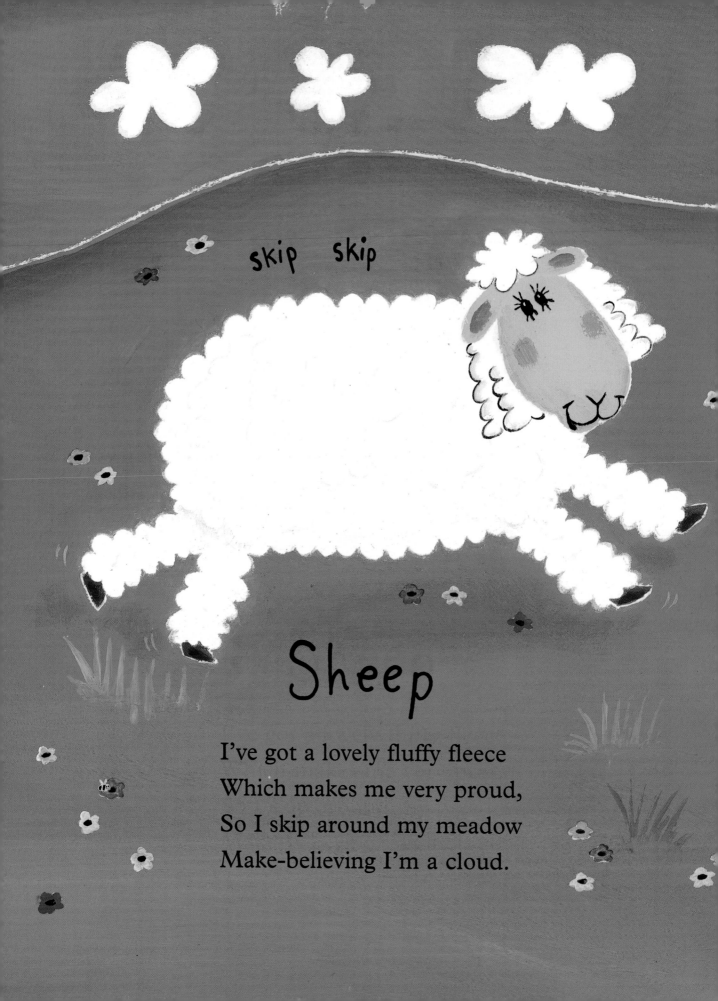

skip   skip

Sheep

I've got a lovely fluffy fleece
Which makes me very proud,
So I skip around my meadow
Make-believing I'm a cloud.

Goat

I sometimes hang out by the sheep-pen
Chortling into my beard.
Sheep often think that they're better than us
But goats never need to get sheared!

chortle! chortle!

clippety clop !

Cart horse

There's nothing like hay when you're hungry,
It's lovely to munch a whole bale,
But sometimes I stop
For a clippety-clop
Or to flick a few flies with my tail.

Bull

I love to snort steam from my nostrils,
It makes me look angry and tough,
And then I start scraping my hoof on the ground
If that isn't scary enough.

Fox

I wait in the woods until nightfall,
Then down to the farmyard I creep,
Because nothing looks quite as delicious
As chickens who've fallen asleep.

creep
creep!

Owl

I always hunt at night time
And I sleep throughout the day.
"Ter-wit, ter-woo," you'll hear me cry,
Out searching for my prey.

ter-wit
ter-woo

Now it's night time on the farmyard,
And the moon is shining bright.
It's time to leave the animals
And wave them all goodnight.

The cows are feeling drowsy
So they settle on the ground.
It won't be very long now
Till they're sleeping safe and sound.

The horse is in his stable
And the hens are in their shed,
But the sheepdog's fallen fast asleep
Inside the farmer's bed!